A BAD
CASE OF
TINNITUS

TONY EVANS

Dark Holler Press is owned and operated by Tony Evans.
Dark Holler Press logo and all related artwork copyright © 2021 by Tony Evans. All rights reserved.

First Edition © 2022 Tony Evans | Dark Holler Press
Cover & Book design by: A. A. Medina | Fabled Beast Design
Editing by: Tony Evans and Ali Sweet

Dark Holler Press #05
ISBN: 9798839755130

www.tonyevanshorror.com
Twitter: @tonyevanshorror
Instagram: @tonyevanshorror

For JWC and Nick "FlapJacks" Poncio.

You better be ridin' in the Oldsmobile for this one, baby! It's a wild one!

#iaintcumyet

"Your country and mine is an interesting one, but there is nothing there that is half so interesting as the human mind."

Mark Twain, *Letters from Earth: Uncensored Writings*, 1962

PART I

HYPOCHONDRIA AND PARANOIA TAKE HOLD

I

THE FIRST THING THAT POPPED INTO ARNOLD MASTERSON'S mind when he heard the strange ringing in his ear was that he had a brain tumor. After all, isn't that the most *common* and *logical* explanation for one to hear a ringing in their ear?

Sure it is. It has to be a tumor. At least, that's what Arnold's fucked up brain was telling him. It happened all the time. Day and night. Didn't matter where he was or what he was doing, whether he was in the presence of large crowds or in a locked room all alone...that goddamn ringing sound was always there. It had come on so suddenly, too, just dropped in out of the clear blue sky.

That *goddamn* ringing!

Well, it was a ringing at first, anyway, and to make it even more noteworthy to his constantly over paranoid mind, it was only happening in his right ear. A constant and nagging buzz that made it hard for him to hear anything else clearly. Just an ever-present sort of dull, almost vibrating hum, that made him feel as if someone were placing one of those handheld vibrating massagers against the base of his skull. It didn't hurt, so that was a plus, but it was starting to make him feel like an old man, and *that,* in particular, annoyed him.

"Well, Mary," Arnold said to his wife. "It looks like I've got a brain tumor. *Fuck!*"

"What?" Mary uttered, paying him little to no attention at all. She was watching television in the other room. One of those countless and overplayed *reality* shows about some group of supposed *real* housewives. "Did you say something, Arnie?"

He scowled quietly at the response.

Arnie. Who the fuck calls anyone Arnie?

He hated that name, which, he reasoned, was why Mary used it. The only other person to ever call him *Arnie* on a regular basis was his mother, and she'd died years ago. "Yeah. I said I've got a brain tumor. Internet says so. That's gotta be what it is causing this noise. It's the most reasonable, logical, and probable explanation, considering everything else." With a half-hearted chuckle... half-hearted because he *kinda sorta* really *did* believe it, as the internet had actually listed that as one potential cause...he looked to her and smiled. "I mean, I guess it *could* be something else. You never can tell about these things, right?" He scrolled further down the page, scanning the various resources available on what he liked to call the 'interweb' for more information. "Some of these websites say that loud noises and even some medicines can cause it, too. They also don't just call it ringing. I guess the real name for it is *tinnitus*."

"Mhm. That's good, Arnie," Mary replied absentmindedly as she watched some jacked up rich husband strutting his stuff on the television for the whole world to see.

"That's good? What do you mean *that's good*? I could have a tumor for Christ's sake."

The shrillness of Arnold's tone pulled Mary away just enough for a somewhat genuine response this time, though her concentration was still largely on the well-built, rich husband. "What are you talking about?"

Arnold was silent for a moment, his mind going a million different directions.

"Arnold!" Mary called, her eyes still fixed on the television. "Are you babbling on about your hearing again?" Reluctantly, she turned her head away from the show and glanced in Arnold's direction. "For fuck's sake, would you stop bothering me with that stuff? Can't you see I'm busy here? You don't have a damn tumor."

"Yeah? How can you be so sure about that? You're using your opinion, and I'm goin' off of information from Doctor Google. He's always right, you know…most of the time."

"Doctor Google, huh? Well, I'm no doctor, but I can tell you that you don't have a tumor." She turned back to the screen. The man she'd been watching was arguing with his wife now about whether or not one of her friends was 'hot'. An argument that can't be won no matter what the husband says. "I could never get so lucky."

Arnold laughed, but it was genuine this time. Their relationship had gotten to that point. Laughter was the only thing really holding it together, or at least that's how it seemed. They'd never had any children, and their interests had drifted over the years, but laughter and self-deprecation was better than nothing. She was all he had, and he really didn't want to lose her. "Oh, shut up, Mary. You know you love me."

She shot a quick look in his direction, her eyes studying him up and down in a way that was hard to judge whether it was joking or serious. "Do I?" She stared at his balding head, his slightly bulged out gut hanging over the waist of his pants, and raised one eyebrow. "I mean, it's not like I married you for your *looks* or anything."

Arnold sighed, trying not to let the remark get to him, though it did. It always got to him. In high school and college, he'd been a totally different person. He'd been fit, in shape, a prime example of an all-star athlete you'd expect to see in one of those really cheesy teenage love movies. But, as it does with all living things, time had taken its toll on him. The years had added weight and flab to his once chiseled physique and time had laid claim to what had once been a thick, full head of hair, stripping it away to nothing more than a strange assortment of randomly placed patches that reminded him of a mangy dog. And to make things worse, age had amplified every ache and pain, no matter how minor, into nothing less than pure unadulterated agony.

Time had not been kind to Arnold. Not at all. But there was no going back now. Just one of those things he had to get used to and accept. Mary, on the other hand, had aged extremely well. She was still just as gorgeous as the day they'd met. Even more attractive, actually. He often wondered why she even stayed with him, especially since she rarely even looked at him anymore, let alone showed interest in him sexually.

"Listen, Arnie. Instead of bothering me about it, why don't you just go get it looked at? God knows that'd be better than pestering me constantly. I'd be willing to bet it's just allergies or something. Maybe an ear infection. Did Doctor Google tell you that?"

Arnold kept scrolling the computer screen, eyes squinted as he read. "I don't know about that. It doesn't hurt or anything like it says it's supposed to with an infection, and it doesn't really feel stopped up. You'd think that an infection would feel stopped up."

She rolled her eyes and went back to watching her show.

"It's strange. It's almost like I can hear *better* out of the one that's bothering me." He closed his laptop and took a deep breath. He knew that the best thing to do was listen to his wife and have it looked at. Even if she didn't really care and was just saying it so he would shut up, an examination by a real doctor would definitely be better than reading some random shit on the internet. But there was always a certain level of anxiety and fear that went with that. What if it really did turn out to be something bad? Then he may potentially be faced with thoughts of surgery or death, or something even worse. He may be stuck having to pay a huge hospital bill, the result of which would inevitably lead to uncontrollable and unbearable financial burden and stress.

No sir, he thought. *To hell with that. No sense in*

adding even more pressure to my already tight wallet strings.

Her show over, Mary walked into the kitchen and stood in front of him, hands on hips. "Well?"

"Well what?"

She was giving him *the* look now. Not the *I'm concerned for you* look, though. This one was the *just fucking do it and stop bugging me about it* look. "You gonna call Doctor Roberts, or you want me to do it for you? Hell, I do everything else around here. I'm surprised you know how to tie your own shoes."

"Oh, for cryin' out loud, Mary. I'm fin—"

She took a step closer and dropped her head, looking at him as if he were a child being disciplined by an angry parent. "I don't want to have to listen to you whine about what it *might* be. It's getting really annoying, Arnold. You all but ruined my show. Now have it looked at. Otherwise, you won't have to worry about whether or not it's a tumor. If I have to hear about it one more time, I'll kill you myself."

"Fine," he grumbled, shaking his head. "I'll call him. Stop treating me like a goddamn baby, would you?"

"Sure…if you stop acting like one. Like I said," she glanced at him again. The way her face looked, it was almost as if she was *hoping* for it to be a tumor, or something else along those lines. "It's not a tumor. Luck is never on my side."

"Thanks, Mary." He sighed, a sarcastic tone evident. "Maybe you'll get *lucky*, as you say, and it'll be some kind of damn brain eating bug that crawled in there and started eating away while I was asleep."

Mary went back into the living room and

plopped down on the couch. "I doubt it. You'd have to have a brain to start with for that to happen. Besides, what kind of bug would want to eat *that*? Just *look* at what it's inside of."

"Ha! Again with the looks, huh?" He picked up the phone and walked over to the refrigerator to get the doctor's number off the emergency list they kept posted on the door.

"You know I'm right," she said. "You just don't want to admit it."

2

THERE'S JUST ONE SMALL THING ABOUT BRAIN EATIN' bugs that you gotta remember, Arnold." Doctor Roberts tugged on Arnold's right earlobe and stuck the pointy end of the otoscope inside. He moved it around a bit, making sure to inspect every square inch of his ear canal.

"Yeah? What's that?"

The doctor chuckled. "That kinda thing just don't live around here."

Arnold sat still while his ear was being looked at. "Not that we know of, that is."

Doctor Roberts pulled away and smiled. "No, that's not what I mean. They don't occur around here at all."

Arnold smirked. "If you say so."

"Let me ask you a few questions. You say it's a ringing, right?"

"Well, it started off as a ringing, yeah. But it's more like a humming or buzzing now. Kinda like a vibration, maybe? And it really comes and goes, sort of."

"Mhm, I see." He squinted his eyes a bit, a gesture that made Arnold nervous. "Can you still hear? Does it feel like it's blocked or stopped up in any way? Muffled or rough, maybe?"

"No. It's the complete opposite, actually. It's almost like I can hear better out of that side. I have to keep it plugged with cotton, too. If I don't it drives me crazy. Like the eardrum is going into overdrive or something."

"Interesting."

Arnold shifted position and swallowed hard, his nervousness making itself known. "Interesting? What's interesting about that? Does that mean it's something bad?"

Doctor Roberts stared at him, his lips tight. "I'll be honest with you, Arnold. Your ears look fine from the outside. Both of 'em do. Fit as a fiddle, in fact. Besides, if you had something in your ear canal, you know...something like a brain eatin' bug for example, it'd really mess with your hearing. You'd be dizzy by now, probably wouldn't even be able to stand up. Plus, it'd hurt like hell. Think about it, it'd be in there chompin' your eardrum to bits. You understand?"

"Yeah, I guess that makes sense."

"And another thing about it is, people don't experience tinnitus...uhm, the technical term for a ringing in the ears—"

"Yeah, I saw that on the internet," Arnold interrupted.

The doctor smiled. "I'm sure you did. Anyway, people don't typically experience that sensation from problems in the ear canal. You see, that sorta thing is usually rooted in the inner or middle ear. It's all behind the eardrum. I can't exactly see back there from out here."

His breathing became rapid and shallow, sweat covered his forehead. "You mean it's all in my brain? Y…you mean I've got a brain tumor? Jesus Christ, I knew it. I knew I was right. Just wait 'til I tell Mary. I knew the internet was right."

Doctor Roberts laughed quietly, his hand held in front of him in a calming manner. "Easy now, Arnold. I didn't say that."

"You said that stuff like this is usually rooted in the brain! What more needs to be said? Sounds pretty self-explanatory to me."

"No, I didn't say that. What I *did* say, was that the cause for things like this is usually located *behind the ear drum*. I didn't say anything about a tumor at all. Sounds like you've been lookin' at one too many medical websites."

"Hey, don't knock the internet. There's a lot of valuable information on there."

"Oh? Seems like you were in here a few months ago trying to convince me that your sore throat was gonorrhea. Do you remember that? And if I recall, it was Doctor Google that gave you that valuable nugget of information, as well."

Arnold blushed. He had, in fact, done just that. But it was only because of the big white pustules on his tonsils. It had looked the same as the pictures he'd seen of diagnosed cases of sexually transmitted disease in patient's throats. "Okay, then. If it's not a tumor, what's causing it? It's about to drive me insane, especially on the bad days."

"To be honest, I'm not sure. Could be a lot of things."

"So…it *could* be a tumor?"

He shook his head. "Technically, it *could* be one, yes. But it's *very* unlikely. Those sorts of tumors, those associated with the inner ear, are pretty rare." He opened up a chart and skimmed through the information on the sheets. "You *are* getting up there in age, you know." His finger came to rest part way down the page. "If my information is correct, you're close to forty-five years old. It's no myth that a body's hearing starts to go with age, Arnold. I've known you for a good many years. We used to listen to music pretty loud in our younger days, remember? That definitely doesn't help."

"Ha! So, you mean to tell me that I wasted my time and money today just so you could tell me that I'm getting old? Hell, I've known that for a while now! Thanks a lot, *Doc*."

"Not exactly. Your ears look fine from the outside. Like I said, perfect, actually. You don't even have that much wax in there. But I'd like to take an x-ray, just to help ease your mind a bit regarding your tumor theory. The next step would be setting up an appointment with a specialist, maybe even get an MRI depending on what they say."

"Specialist? What kind of specialist?"

"An ear, nose, and throat specialist. They see a lot more cases of this type of stuff than a family doctor like myself ever will. They study it, specialize in it, and they have the tools and instruments to see what I can't. Plus, they know a little more about what to look for."

"Mhm. And I bet they charge a shitload more than you, too."

"Oh, don't worry, Arnold." He walked over and patted his friend on the back. "This visit will be on the house. You know, since we're such good friends and all."

Arnold jerked back, his brow arching. "Oh... well, I mean, you don't have to—"

"Seriously, Arnold, don't worry about it. But, if it *does* turn out to be a tumor, I expect every bit of your business from then on. Got it?"

"Oh, of course. Yeah, one hundred percent."

"But, we'll still do an x-ray first. That way you can take it with you to the specialist and they won't charge you for that bit. It'll be a little easier on the pocket. We'll call you on Monday with the results, and I'll give you a referral at that time. Try to forget about it 'til then. Can you do that?"

"Monday? Jesus, man. How am I supposed to wait until Monday? You know me. I'm paranoid as hell about this stuff!"

"I'm not sure, Arnold. Maybe the brain tumor will make you forget about it by then?"

Arnold let out a huge snort as he chuckled. "You know...you're okay for a doctor. You're nowhere near as big an asshole as everyone says."

Doctor Roberts laughed and patted Arnold's shoulder. "Sounds like I need to do somethin' different then. I'll try to be a little meaner in the future, since I have such a reputation to uphold."

3

AS ARNOLD LAY IN BED THAT NIGHT, HE DID EXACTLY what his good friend, Doctor John Roberts, had instructed him *not* to do. He thought about a tumor in his brain.

He thought about it a lot, actually. It was impossible not to. The ringing was constant, and it seemed to get worse after the doctor's visit. There was absolutely nothing he could do to make it stop, and he'd tried just about everything he could think of. Sure, covering his head with a pillow and pressing it against his ear seemed to help a *little*, but sill, it rang on.

He flopped over to his left side and slid the pillow down over his head. He thought about what Doctor Roberts had said about how no brain eating bugs lived in Kentucky. One thing he knew, though, was that science was advancing at an alarming rate, and people had been wrong before. Hell, when he was in middle school his science teacher told the entire class that black widow spiders didn't live in eastern Kentucky either. Arnold knew better than that and he didn't care what any old field guide or other book or science teacher had to say about it. He'd seen them, and that's all it took! So, he caught one from under a cinderblock next to an old shed outside of his house and took it in, making the teacher out to look like an idiot.

What if this was something similar? What if Arnold would somehow prove medical science wrong?

Or worse. What if some lab had been conducting experiments, the government even, using a particularly nasty variety of the brain hungry insect as a means to destroy the minds of the United States of America's worst enemies? What if they were planning to use said insects to fight wars and chew away the brain tissue of anyone seeking to cause the country harm? What if one of the secret insectoid weapons had somehow escaped and found a home deep inside of his skull, crawled in one night while he was sound asleep and just started munching away until it hit the part of his brain responsible for hearing in his right ear?

Arnold chuckled at the thought. It *was* a pretty ridiculous scenario, after all. He took a few deep breaths, exhaling each slowly as he tried to put it out of his mind and think of other things to occupy his thoughts. Positive things, things that would maybe help him relax instead of freak the fuck out. He thought of the day he'd met Mary. She always made him smile. She was his everything, despite how he was sure she felt about him nowadays. He thought about how beautiful she was, about how proud his father had been that he'd found such a lovely woman to take care of him. Too bad she didn't seem to give a damn anymore, let alone love him.

She'd never just up and said it, but sometimes things like that are best left untouched. She didn't have to say it. He knew it to be true. He could just feel it, the distinct lack of caring in her voice when she spoke to him, the way she always seemed pre-occupied with anything else, even when he was speaking directly to her. It was as obvious as it could be without smacking him right in the face. And the worst part was that he couldn't really blame her. But he still loved her, and those early memories helped him to calm down. Besides, he'd be dead, eventually, and any time spent with some-one as perfect as Mary, whether she loved him or not, was certainly better than being alone.

He grinned and remembered those early times in their relationship again, and before long he be-gan to drift off into a deep sleep.

Then he heard the first voice.

It was low in volume and more like something or someone mumbling, but the only thing his tired brain registered was that it sounded like a voice.

"Hu...wha...?" Arnold mumbled. He jerked his head up and glanced over to Mary. She looked to be unconscious, but she'd been known to talk in her sleep from time to time. "Keep it down, would you? I'm tryin' to sleep." He shifted position a bit and rested his head back on the pillow.

The sound came again, slightly louder, and less like a mumble.

This time, it was clearly a voice. Someone whispering.

Arnold lay there, eyes closed, a small shot of adrenaline pumped into his bloodstream as he tried to reconcile if he was really hearing something or if it was all in his imagination.

Another whisper. This one so crisp and clear that there was no mistaking it.

"Hey, wake up, *dick*. I ain't got time to be fuckin' around. We've got work to do."

Arnold raised his head slowly and glanced back to his wife. "Mary, seriously, if you're playing some kind of joke, it's getting old. I'm trying to get some rest. Please, be quie—"

"It's not Mary you fucking moron. Goddamn. Has her voice ever sounded like this?"

Arnold paused for a brief moment, unsure of what to do or what was happening.

"That's right, lay there and look all confused, dumbass. That'll do it. Just shut the fuck up and stop talking or you're gonna wake her, and neither of us need that shit. Am I right? I mean, Jesus H. Christ! You know how she gets when you disturb her."

A sudden surge of fear jolted Arnold's body into overdrive. His eyes flew open as he sat up, jostling the whole bed. "What the fuck?" he said, short of breath from the rushing adrenaline. He looked at Mary again. She was there in bed next to him, sound asleep. His eyes wide, he shook his head slowly, even more confused as he watched her lips for any sign of movement. It had to be her. *Had* to be. Otherwise…

But there was no movement on her lips. None at

all. There was no sound other than that of her long, slow breathing.

"That's better," the voice said. "At least *you're* awake now. Small steps, right? Isn't that what you guys say? Take it one step at a time or some shit? Fuck, I don't know. I've never understood your kind."

Arnold's brain was racing. He was losing his mind. He *had* to be. He was hearing voices now... voices from people who weren't there.

What the fuck is happening to me?

"Okay, now get up and go to the bathroom. Just please, for the love or God, make sure to shut the door behind you. That old bitch doesn't need to see or hear any part of what's about to happen. I mean, unless you want her to have a goddamn heart attack, that is. Hell, the way she treats you, though, that might not be such a bad thing." The voice chuckled.

Arnold stared at his wife's mouth blankly as he tried to make sense of what was happening. He looked around the room frantically. As far as he could tell, there was no one else there with them. It *was* dark though. He supposed that it wasn't that far out of the realm of possibility for someone to be hiding behind the door. He'd heard stranger stories on the news. He could feel his heartbeat increasing and that familiar metallic taste covered his tongue as the thought of an intruder sunk in, climaxing to a level that left his hands shaking and his lungs short of breath. He turned to the side and started to place his feet on the floor when an even more intrusive thought hit him.

Wait a minute. What if there's some pervert hiding

under the bed? Some fucked up weirdo just waiting to grab me. He could be waiting to lick my toes or…

He jerked his feet up and nearly fell backward onto Mary, shaking the whole bed again in the process.

Mary stirred a bit, her tongue sliding gently between her lips moistening them. She mumbled something about Brian's muscles and how they were so hard and strong and stiff.

Arnold paused. *What? Brian…from her work? Why the fuck is she talking about Brian?*

"Really?" he heard the strange voice say. "You're worse than a little kid, and trust me, I know. I've scared quite a few of them in my days. Comes with the territory, you know?" The voice laughed. "You really think I'm under the fucking bed? Goddamn, son! You *are* one stupid son-of-a bitch, aren't you?"

Arnold wasn't sure what to do. First of all, the lingering question of who the fuck was talking to him and where the fuck they were was still very much out there in the open. Was there someone watching him? Watching his every move only to criticize everything he decided to do? Because that's what it seemed like. If so, why was the sound of the voice not waking Mary? Could she not hear it? It was certainly loud enough for him to hear, so surely, she could hear it, too. And secondly, though not as important at this very moment in time, but important to Arnold and his sanity nonetheless… why the fuck was Mary talking about Brian in her sleep?

Carefully, Arnold pushed himself back to a seated position and lowered his feet to the floor with extreme caution. He thought about what he'd do if a hand were to actually shoot out and grab his ankle. Would he scream like a frightened little child? Would he fight them? Would he be forced to defend himself, to defend Mary, and his home against what would surely be deemed the prowling neighborhood foot licking menace?

Perhaps, if he knew how to fight, that would be an option. Maybe *Brian* would come to rescue them. He'd rescue Mary at the very least. Maybe that's what she really wanted. If it was the same Brian he was thinking of, he *was* pretty muscular.

Arnold scowled. *Huge, hard, stiff muscles.*

Brian was most definitely better suited to fighting than Arnold. In truth, Arnold would probably run, or at least that would be his first impulse. But he could never leave Mary in danger. No matter what. He'd have to try.

"Hey," the voice said. "Are you gonna get goin' or what?"

"Oh," Arnold whispered. "Y…yeah. Hold on." He raised his hand to the side of his head and stuck his right pinky finger in his ear. Something was itching deep in his ear canal, the same ear that had been bothering him. He rooted around a bit, jerking his finger back and forth, and as he removed it, an overwhelming sensation struck him. "I'll be *damned.* The ringing, I…it's almost completely gone."

"Well woopty-fuckin' do," the strange voice said. "The ringing in your ear stopped. Big fuckin' deal. What, you want it to start again? Here, let me help with that."

Out of nowhere, a sharp pain shot through Arnold's head like a lightning bolt and the ringing came hard and fast, worse than ever. Arnold cupped his hands over his ears, as the sound made him dizzy. He gritted his teeth and shook his head, but nothing seemed to work. Then, as suddenly as it had started, the ringing stopped again.

"There, pussy," the voice grunted. "Now, listen to me this time or I'll do it again, only it'll be much worse!"

"How did you…how did you know that my ear was ringing? How did you do that?"

"Shhh! For cryin' out loud, man! How many times am I gonna have to tell you to keep your god-damn voice down? If you wake your wife up, we'll both be fucked. And not in the way that you wanna be fucked, either. We'll be *fucked* as in a *giant ass red dick that shoots flames from its tip as it's forcing its way into every hole both of us have* kind of fucked. Got it?"

Arnold jumped to his feet and stared into the darkness. Confusion definitely played a major role in his current state of mind as it sunk its claws deep into his tired mind. Convinced that he was either going crazy or that someone was hiding in the room, he went to the door and checked behind it. Nothing. He went to the closet and slowly opened it. Still, nothing.

"What in the world is happening to me?"

"Look," the voice whispered. "I really didn't want to do this, but I had no other choice in the matter. You've gotta trust me on that. You think I like it in here?"

"What do you mean, *in here*?"

"Quiet! Damn, man. I'll explain everything to you later. I promise. But you've got to do what I say first. Understand?"

Before he responded, Arnold stopped himself,

realizing that if he answered a voice that he couldn't see – one that, based on all the evidence he had before him other than the fact that he himself could hear it, wasn't even there – he just may have to admit to himself that he was going off the deep end.

Oh, I get it! This is all a dream. Yeah…yeah! It has to be. What else could explain it?

Arnold thought about the odds of such a crazy dream for a moment, and swiftly came up with one fatal flaw to the explanation. He'd never had such a wild and crazy dream in his life. Nothing that felt *this* real. Sure, there's a first time for everything, and he *had* eaten some spicy food right before bed…but still, he'd never dreamt anything like this before.

Luckily, there was a tried-and-true method for testing a theory such as this; a method that always worked. Well, at least in the movies. Arnold closed his eyes and reached his hand up to his face. Taking a chunk of his cheek between forefinger and thumb, he pinched down hard as if trying to pop a massive pimple. It took a minute for the pain to transmit from his skin to his brain, but when it did, he couldn't help but to shout.

"Jesus Christ!" he belted, jerking his face back. "That wasn't supposed to hurt! This is *supposed* to be a goddamn dream!"

"Huh? Arnold? Th…that you?"

He shot a glance over to Mary who was now shifting around under the covers.

"Now you've gone and done it *stupid*!" the voice scolded.

"Oh, uhm, yeah. I'm just…" He paused briefly as he thought about asking her who Brian was and if it was the same Brian she was always working late with, but considering everything else that was going on at the moment, he decided against it. It could wait. The voice, or whatever it was, was more important right now. "...going to the bathroom."

He froze, waiting for her to respond. He wasn't quite sure why he was so worried about it. So what if she woke up? It wasn't like he was doing anything wrong. Waking up in the middle of the night to take a piss wasn't illegal. It was actually normal for God's sake. He was getting older. Old people go to the bathroom a lot.

But the voice, the whisper said he'd get it if she were to wake up. And *it* wasn't any ordinary disciplining either. Not according to the voice, anyway. Apparently, *it* was a giant flaming dick that would get rammed in and out of every hole he had.

Arnold winced at the thought. Nothing at *all* about that scenario sounded fun in any way. It was just a voice, though, right? Those threats couldn't have any weight to them. Could they?

Luckily, Arnold wouldn't have to find out just yet. Mary hadn't woken up. He could tell by the sounds of her snoring, which were cutting through the air like razors. She'd always told him that she didn't snore, and he'd always argued that point with her, a thought that put a smile of arrogance on his otherwise concerned face. Right now, she was most certainly *sawing some logs*, as the old saying goes.

"Good," the voice said. "Now, do like you told her and get to the fucking bathroom before you actually wake her up!"

"But—"

"Go!"

The ringing in his ear came back with a vengeance. It was as if it were being used as some sort of cruel and unethical disciplinary method, like a shock collar on a disobedient dog, by a ruthless and uncaring trainer. A trainer who strangely had the ability to zap him at will, even though he wasn't wearing a collar.

"Holy-o-okay, okay," he whispered, both hands on either side of his head trying to calm the piercing sound. "For cryin' out loud. Just make it stop!"

"Whathe…" Mary mumbled, turned over, and pulled the covers over her head.

The sound in his ear died back to a more tolerable level and he quickly stumbled into the bathroom, closing the door behind him. He squinted for a moment, his hand on his brow shielding his eyes from the sudden change in brightness as he flipped the light switch. There was a bright red spot on his cheek, surrounded by two small crescent shaped marks, where his fingernails had dug in earlier. He ran his fingers over the abrasion. It was real, alright. Nothing *dream like* about it, and it was gonna leave one hell of a bruise in the morning.

"What in the hell was I thinking," Arnold whispered to himself. "Should've known better. I guess shit like that only works in the movies." He ran his fingers over his balding head and took in a deep breath, listening for the voice to start back up. The ringing had remained at a constant but mostly tolerable level. Otherwise, everything was still and quiet.

He shook his head at his reflection in the mirror and snorted. The whole thing was comical, really. What else could he say? It must've been a dream after all. He opened the medicine cabinet and grabbed a cotton ball, stuffing a small chunk of it into his ear. He turned around to flip the light off and open the door when an abrupt itching deep in his head nearly caused him to fall. Arms out, he wobbled back and forth before finally clutching the wall for stability. He shook his head wildly and pressed his right palm against his ear, jerking it around in an attempt to scratch the sudden itch.

*It's a goddamn brain eating bug! I knew it! God-*damn *that fuckin' doctor!*

He closed his eyes and knelt down, hoping it would ease the dizziness, and as he did, a faint chuckle crept closer in the background. A piercing pain engulfed his ear again, this time spreading over the entire right side of his face. Something was moving in there. He could feel it. Something was maneuvering around, wiggling maybe, deep in his ear canal, trying to force its way out. He pushed harder against his face to try and stifle the pain, but it was no use. It just intensified, increasing in severity from the inside as his entire head started throbbing.

He stood up and fumbled toward the sink, taking another look in the mirror. His breathing increased as panic set in, a light coating of sweat glazed his forehead. He rummaged around for a tweezer, but the pain made his focus weak. He saw a bobby pin next to the toothpaste and grabbed it instead. He reached for the cotton in his ear, but just before his fingers made contact, it popped out on its own accord. But it didn't just fall, it launched from inside of his ear and flew across the room in an explosive jump, as if it'd all of a sudden sprouted legs and leaped in an attempt to save itself from a burning building.

Arnold didn't care about all that, though. Not right now. Whatever was happening inside of his head had reached near unbearable levels. He reared back and plunged the bobby pin toward the opening of his ear, bracing himself for a sharp gouge.

But there was no gouge. Nothing of the sort. Instead, something crazy happened.

A tiny little hand reached out and grasped the bobby pin, preventing its entry.

Arnold stared at it in the mirror, his mouth hanging open like a surprised child. He couldn't believe what he was seeing. "Holy fucking shit. That's a little bitty hand!"

PART II

EXIT, STAGE... OR EAR?...RIGHT

4

IT WASN'T A NORMAL SIZED HAND BY ANY STRETCH OF THE IMAGINATION. It was much smaller, the size of a child's action figure, and it was attached to an arm of equally similar proportion.

Arnold gasped in horror as the tiny appendage wiggled back and forth, pulling against the bobby pin like it was fighting for control. He pulled against the tiny hand's hold, and every time he did the arm attached to it dragged out a little further. "Wh...what the fuck is this!"

He started to tremble, his belief in what his eyes were seeing had started to dissolve rapidly. The pain was still there, and it was, in fact, rather excruciating, but the sight of an actual hand, a goddamned miniature fucking hand and arm, being pulled from his ear was dulling all of his other senses.

He continued to pull, and eventually an elbow emerged, followed by a shoulder, and that's when he was finally met with a stronger resistance. Until that point, the miniscule appendage had slithered out with relative ease, a light coating of wax and blood helping to lubricate it along its journey.

Arnold dropped the bobby pin and staggered backward. "H…holy shit," he mumbled, voice trembling.

"Hey! What the hell do you think you're doing?" The voice he heard was no longer a whisper; it had morphed into a full-on yell, though quieter than the normal yell of a full-sized person. It was like the words were coming from a smaller version of something human-*like*, but not quite fully human. "Get hold of my hand, would you? Kinda hard to get any traction from this position with all this wax and blood and shit. Don't you ever clean your god-damn ears? Just *pull*!"

"Wh-I-I don't…"

"Yeah, yeah. I know. Look, I get it, really, I do. You don't know what's happening. You're wondering if you're going crazy…if you're really seeing a little arm come out of your ear. You're not the first person to have questioned these things, believe me. I know."

Arnold fell to his butt, his entire body quivering from both mental and physical exhaustion. His eyes wide, his head throbbed painlessly as adrenaline continued to course through his bloodstream, numbing his pain receptors. "I-is this…no, i-it *can't* be real. I mean, can it? What the fuck is going on here? Wh…what *are* you?"

"I'd be happy to tell you, if you could just help

me out a little, maybe?"

Reluctantly, Arnold took hold of the tiny hand and started to pull. "It's stuck. I mean, *you're* stuck?"

The thing laughed. "Yeah, just pull harder. Give it a good tug. But be warned. It's gonna hurt like hell, and you're liable to see quite a bit of blood before you —"

Before the voice had a chance to finish, Arnold took in a deep breath and jerked the arm like a parent trying to pull their child from the jaws of a hungry alligator. He heard a loud *pop* and felt an immense pain course through his head as he crashed to the floor.

The hand slid from between his fingers and something splatted against the far wall echoing a dull, yet squishy sound. His entire body shaking, Arnold pushed himself up on hands and knees and scanned the room. Blood was dripping from his right ear into an already formed puddle the size of a large pancake. His eyes narrowed, he looked toward the wall and saw blood splatter there, and just below the stain, there was something small and red squirming around on the tile floor.

It jumped to its feet and stretched a pair of arms and legs, a quiet groan of pleasure radiating throughout the small space. "That's *much* better," it said, then walked over to Arnold and knelt in front of him, directly below his face. "Allow me to introduce myself. My name is Arraleg. It's a pleasure to *formally* meet you, Arnold Masterson."

Arnold tried to speak, but he was too scared and weak to form any type of coherent sentence. He swayed back and forth on his knees, his mouth moving but no sound coming out. He just stared at Arraleg like he was some kind of make-believe *thing*.

And maybe he was.

No more than six inches tall, the little thing stood with his hands behind his back, a polite and direct posture. He walked on two feet, just like any average sized human Arnold had ever known, but he had a long tail that looked to be tipped in some sort of sharp, triangular instrument. His chin was long and drawn out, the very tip covered in a small patch of course black hair. From what Arnold could tell in his tired and weary state, each of the little thing's feet had only two toes, both with long, pointed claws. His skin appeared to be a crimson, almost scarlet red, though it was near to impossible to tell if that was the actual color or if he was just caked in a thick layer of blood.

"It's okay, Arnold. I know this is all a lot to take in."

Arnold nodded.

Arraleg took a glance around the room. There was a pool of blood on the floor, a trail of it leading from Arnold to the wall. "It looks like there's a bit of a mess here to clean up, huh?"

Arnold fell to his side and tried to speak. "D-dnt…ndrstnd." The adrenaline had started to wear off and the throbbing in his head was beginning to hurt again.

"You will," Arraleg told him.

"Arnold? Are you still in the bathroom? Are you okay in there?" Mary called out.

"Fuck! Well, I'll explain as soon as I can. Right now, I've gotta get this shit clean and get out of sight." He held his hands up in the air and began to whisper in a language that Arnold couldn't understand. But he really didn't need to understand it. Like something straight out of one of those old made for television magic shows, he watched the blood on the floor and the wall pulled away from each surface and hovered in mid-air, small droplets of scarlet shaded rain that suspended above Arraleg. He began to spin his hand like a cowboy readying to lasso a bull and the droplets of blood followed suit, clinging together until they formed a small whirlpool in the air. "Open up, Arnold. It's down the hatch with your own mess."

"What?" Arnold said, confused.

As his mouth opened to speak, Arraleg slung his arm like a pitcher throwing a fastball. The blood flew toward Arnold, slipping between his lips and down into his throat. He coughed once as the metallic taste covered his tongue.

"Oh, yeah." Arraleg snapped his fingers and smiled. "There, that should help with the pain."

Arnold opened his eyes with ease as both the throbbing and the pain in his skull came to an abrupt halt.

"Say nothing of me to her. Do you understand? I'll be back shortly. And remember…it's the big red cock if you do!" Arraleg leaped up on the side of the bathtub and ran to hide between the shower curtains.

Arnold tried to look up at him, but as he did, the bathroom door flung open and slammed into his head. The pain returned, but only for a moment as he slipped into unconsciousness.

5

RNOLD FELT A STINGING WARMTH SPREAD ACROSS HIS FACE.
Not a *warmth*, per se; not like when something
heats up. It was more like a sudden explosion
of pain accompanied by a loud smacking sound.
He could hear a voice, too, but it was muffled and
distant. Everything around him was dark, and the
voice seemed to be getting closer. Another loud
smack with that same feeling of searing pain in his
face, and suddenly a flicker of light entered his vi-
sion. It took him a moment to realize what was happening, but when the voice became clear enough to
recognize, it was blatantly obvious.

He opened his eyes and saw the tiled floor of the
bathroom, his wife standing above him. He briefly
caught a glimpse of her arm stretched back like a
catapult, her hand open wide and flat as she hurled
it toward his face.

"Arnold? What happened?"

His eyes widened to comical proportions. Luck, at least in this particular instance on this particular day, was on Arnold Masterson's side. He was able to move his head out of the way just in time to avoid getting smacked by Mary for a third time. Like a prized fighter, his head zipped to the side and lowered slightly, bobbing and weaving with great agility. "What in the hell are you doing?" he shouted.

Mary grabbed his shoulders and shook him. "Are you okay? Do I need to call 911?"

Arnold reached for her hands, freeing himself of her hold. "If you don't stop shaking me, yeah. You're gonna give me whiplash for God's sake. What's wrong with you? And who the fuck is *Brian*?"

She stepped back, one hand on her hip, the other held to her side palm up, a partially confused and horrified look on her face. "Brian? Wh…what do you, B…Brian who? From work you mean?"

"Yeah, that's what I'd like to know."

Mary blushed and her eyes blinked rapidly. "I…I don't know what you're talking about. I…I don't know…I heard you thumping and thrashing around in here like an idiot. You were causing enough commotion to wake the dead! I thought you might've fallen, which apparently, I was right about, because when I came in you were laying splayed out on the floor. I knocked you on the head with the door. What happened?"

"Well…I—" Arnold froze mid-sentence, confusion setting in. He remembered getting up, and he *vaguely* remembered going in to the bathroom (he definitely remembered hearing her talk about Brian and his hard, stiff muscles, though). But why? He looked around the room, his hand against his aching head. "I can't remember, honestly. I think I had to use the bathroom, maybe?"

Mary sighed, relieved he hadn't mentioned Brian again. "That's the last thing I remember you saying."

"But...I'm not really sure. I remember hearing something about Br —"

"You must've been dreaming or something, Arnold," she said, quick to change the subject.

As he glanced around the room, he caught the smallest movement at the edge of the shower curtain. Like a rush of cold air filling your lungs when you open the car door on a frigid winter day, what happened to him only moments before came rushing back. His heart skipped a beat, forcing him to take a short breath. "O-oh, yeah..." He watched closely as a small head poked out from between the shower curtains, staring at him with a scowl so fierce that it could melt steel.

Arraleg, he thought. *That was real?*

"Arnold?" Mary said. "You're acting kinda strange."

"Yeah...tha...that's right," he stuttered. "I had to pee. Really bad, actually. Then, the funniest thing happened."

She cocked her head to the side, waiting for his explanation. "Oh? Funny, huh? Something so funny that you fell down?" She knelt next to him and placed a hand on his forehead. "You don't have a fever, at least."

He shook his head, shoeing her hand away. "Jesus, Mary. No, I don't have a fever." He looked to the shower again and saw Arraleg standing on the edge of the tub, half of his miniature body exposed, a tiny finger to his lips in a shushing gesture. "I had a dream. At least, I *think* it was a dream."

"You had a dream while you were awake and peeing? This isn't making any sense, Arnold. Not the first bit of it."

"No," he said. "I mean, yeah, I guess…but I can't remember it. I was half asleep, after all. I remember getting up from the toilet…and I must've slipped. Yeah! That's what happened. I think I got a little pee on the floor and I must've slipped on it." He looked at Arraleg again, who was smiling this time, a tiny thumb of approval stuck up in the air.

Mary's eyes narrowed. She looked to the floor in front of the toilet. "Slipped on pee, huh?" She took a step over and placed her bare foot on the ground. "It's all dry here, Arnold."

"Well, I *was* half asleep, you know. Maybe I just dreamed it and lost balance or something."

"Mhm. Sure."

He looked at Mary in a strange way. He could feel the joke coming, and it was coming hard. "What?"

"Oh, nothing. Just thinking of how funny it's gonna be to tell everyone that you went to sleep on the toilet and fell off, but you dreamed that you peed in the floor and fell in it. That's all." She laughed at Arnold and started toward the doorway.

"Aren't you gonna help me get up?"

She glanced back at him, a dead and irritated look in her eyes. "You don't seem to be hurt that badly. You're a big boy. I think you can manage."

"At least you checked on me I guess."

"Yeah, I was afraid you'd make a mess in here and leave it for me to clean up."

6

ARNOLD WAS STILL AWAKE AS THE SUN BROKE THROUGH the bedroom window. Sleep had not been his friend that night. The thought of the little man climbing out of his ear just wouldn't let him rest. He'd ran through every logical explanation at least ten times, and he'd *almost* convinced himself that it was all in his head.

Hearing voices – sure. People hear voices all the time.

Tinnitus – okay! That's a relatively common condition that's caused by tons of things.

Dizziness – absolutely! Comes with age. Vertigo, blood pressure changes, whatever!

But the part that he got hung up on, the part that he just couldn't let go, was the little man. Not once in his life had he *ever* heard of a little man crawling out of the ear of a human being, or of any living thing for that matter. Let alone one with red skin and a goddamn pointed, triangular tipped tail! There was no fucking way it was real.

No. Fucking. Way!

He lay in bed nervously wiggling his feet back and forth. His heart raced as sweat covered his palms. All night had been like this. All *fucking* night.

Mary stretched and let out a groan. Arnold abruptly stopped all movement. He couldn't afford her asking questions about why he was acting so strange (at least he felt like he was acting strange, anyway), and if anyone would pick up on his behavior, it would be her. If she did, he may slip up and mention the little man. Then, she'd think him crazy for sure. Who wouldn't? Plus, she already made enough fun of him for his looks. He didn't need to give her another reason to slaughter his self-esteem any further.

She turned over and saw him lying flat of his back, a look somewhere between scared and confused plastered on his face. She grabbed her phone and began scrolling through all of her different social media accounts, checking the morning gossip.

Arnold scowled. *She's probably checking up on Brian.*

"You okay, Arnold?"

He stiffened. *Am I okay? Of course I'm okay, Mary. Why wouldn't I be okay? Nothing happened. It's not like something fucked up went down in the bathroom in the middle of the goddamn night like a fucking man crawling out of my head or anything.*

"Arnold?" Mary said again, more directly this time.

He jerked suddenly, his hands darting to his sides as if he'd just been woken from a deep sleep.

"Oh, yeah. I'm good." He wiped his hands against the sheets, his feet started fidgeting again. "Just thinking about that dream last night. Crazy, huh?"

Her attention was still on her phone.

Thank God. Dodged the bull —

"Dream, you say? I'm still not sure what all that was about. Didn't you say you forgot the dream?" She looked over at him, a slight bit of concern on her face. Did she have something to hide? It *was* Brian…Arnold *knew* it. "

He was quiet again. Had he mentioned that he couldn't remember? Probably so, but he *hadn't* forgotten. Not at all. The little red man, Arraleg, plagued his thoughts. His lips tight against his teeth, he waited as patiently as possible for Mary to get up. He loved her, yes, but right now he had other things on his mind. First and foremost, he wanted to go to the bathroom and see if the little crimson fucker actually existed.

After a long moment of awkward silence from both of them, Mary stood up. "Well, as long as you're okay, I guess." She started toward the bathroom. Immediately, Arnold's heart leapt into his throat.

He gripped the sheets tightly, a horrible realization struck him. *She can't see him! She can't know he's in there!* "The…the bathroom?" he blurted out. He didn't mean to. Not like that. Saying such a stupid thing would obviously draw attention. That's what normal people do when they wake up from a long night of sleep. They go to the bathroom. He thought as hard and as fast as he could, trying to come up with something to say that wouldn't make him sound completely insane.

Mary stopped in the doorway, giving him an absurd look. "Yeah. The bathroom. Is that a problem?"

"Uhm, no." He struggled for words. He needed something, something that sounded *normal*, not like he was trying to conceal his secret. Anything! Suddenly, it came to him. The simplest and most obvious answer in the world. "I, uhm, I just have to pee really bad."

Mary stared at him, eyebrows raised, grinning slightly. "Yeah, well, I was up first. You can wait. I'll only be a second." She disappeared into the room.

Silence fell over the house. Arnold began to panic. His heart pounded, a wet sheen glistened over his forehead. He could feel himself breathing heavily, near the verge of hyperventilation. He raised upright in the bed and braced his hands on the mattress. "Hey, you about done in there? I really gotta —" Mid-sentence, the sound of rushing water roared from the bathroom. Arnold's eyes widened, he was on high alert now, waiting for Mary to scream at the sight of the thing in there with her. He waited for what seemed like hours, though in reality it couldn't have been more than a few seconds.

"All yours, weirdo," Mary said, standing in the bathroom doorway.

Arnold sprang to his feet, tossing the covers to the side as if they were on fire.

She looked at him and grimaced. "Jesus, Arnold. What's wrong with you?"

"Oh…uhm, nothin…why? What do you mean?"

She shook her head, a mixture of disgust and bewilderment. "Wash yourself off. You look disgusting."

"Yeah, okay. That's a...a good idea. I think I'll take a shower. Yeah. A shower. That's it."

"You do that," she said, and headed into the kitchen.

As she left the room, Arnold ran to the bathroom as if his life depended on it and closed the door behind him. It was time to find out for himself if what he'd experienced last night was real, or if it had just been the product of some crazy and fucked up nightmare.

The first place he looked was the last place he'd remembered seeing him – between the shower curtains. Slowly, he put one hand on each curtain and readied himself to pull the outer one away. His muscles tight, he licked his lips and swallowed hard. He couldn't decide if he wanted to find something or not. The outcome of either reality seemed to be equally ridiculous.

He closed his eyes and began mentally counting to three.

One.

He braced his legs, unsure of what to expect. His heart pounded harder than he could remember it ever pounding before.

Two.

He opened his eyes and took in another deep breath, the thudding in his chest now creeping up into his throat and around the sides of his head.

Three!

In one quick and smooth motion, Arnold yanked the shower curtains apart. "Ah-HA!" he screamed, like some kind of crazed father looking for his child during an intense game of hide and seek.

His breathing was out of control as he stood

there looking down at the side of the bathtub. It was empty. No washcloth. No soap. But most importantly, there was no little red man. He held his breath for a few seconds in an attempt to slow his heart rate; it was now so strong that he could hear it beating in his ears.

Fuck's sake. I guess I did imagine it after all.

He let out a long sigh of relief as the adrenaline started to subside. He reached in and turned on the shower, pulling the curtain closed to prevent spray from getting all over the floor.

All he needed was another slip leading to another knock on the head.

He pulled his pajama pants off and tossed them to the side, then reached for the under-sink cabinet to grab a clean washcloth. As his hand touched the handle, the cabinet door flew open as if something was forcing it from the inside. It flung open fast, like a bomb had been set to go off from within as soon as he touched it. A high-pitched laughter filled the air and the little red Arraleg leaped from the dark space.

"Boo!" he yelled, landing just in front of Arnold and dancing a fancy little jig.

"Holy shit!" Arnold yelped, stumbling back against the door.

The little man laughed wildly. "What? You didn't think I was a dream, did you?" He winked at Arnold and stuck his tongue out; a childish taunt one expects on an elementary school playground.

"You...you're *real*. You're *really* real." Arnold's hand found his chest as he looked down at the little man in disbelief.

"Was that a question or a statement? Oh, doesn't

matter. My response is the same either way. Of course I'm real!"

"I just don't…" He trailed off, unsure of what else to say, or whether saying anything at all would even make a difference.

"I do believe I owe you an explanation," Arraleg said. He jumped up on the sink and had a seat. His legs hanging over the edge, he took his tail in his right hand and twirled it around like a child does with a small section of rope. "Well, for starters, my name is Arraleg."

"Yeah. I remember that part," Arnold replied.

"Oh, well good then. You might wanna brace yourself for the next part, though. It's usually that thing that really fucks with people."

"I think I'm pretty braced," Arnold said, a hint of condescension in his voice. "I mean, you did crawl out of my fucking head last night, right? How much crazier could it get?"

"Okay, suit yourself then. If you're sure."

"Yeah. I'm sure."

"Well, I usually go about this in a more indirect way, but I mostly deal with younger humans. They don't typically have the same intellectual capacity as the older ones of your species. So, in your case, I'll just tell you." Arraleg held his other hand up to his mouth and breathed on his clawed fingers as if proud of what he was about to say. He wiped them against his naked chest and a small grin formed across his face. "Believe it or not, Arnold Masterson, I'm a demon, and even better, in your case at least, I can be of great service to you, *if* you'll allow."

7

ARNOLD WATCHED AS THE LITTLE MAN TWIRLED HIS TAIL. He sat up straight on the edge of the counter, his chest jutted out like a proud little banty rooster. What he'd said made Arnold grin, and he couldn't help but chuckle at the statement. "A demon? Yeah, *sure* you are. Demons aren't real, buddy. I stopped believing in all that shit a *long* time ago."

Arraleg smiled, a set of the whitest and sharpest teeth Arnold had ever seen glistening in the light. "Is that a fact?" He raised his left hand in the air and snapped his thin, pointy fingers. Out of nowhere, a flame sparked on his fingertip. "If I were you, I'd start believing again. That is, if you want to save your everlasting soul from the fiery depths of Hell."

Arnold chuckled. "Really, now? That seems like quite a stretch, doesn't it?"

Arraleg cocked his head to the side, his tail still twirling in his hand.

"I mean, of all the souls in all the world, why would you be here to get mine? There's no way I could be so special that Satan would go out of his way to get little ol' me. And an even bigger question is, why would he send…" he raised his hand to his front, gesturing at Arraleg, "…uh, you?"

"Hey, now. I resent that," Arraleg snapped. "And that's not even how it works. Not in this case, anyway. You see, Satan can be a real asshole from time to time. Hell is a rough place, man. I needed a little break from it all. You know, being a demon is just like any other job when you look at the heart of it. You gotta get up every day and go to work, trying your best to please the big boss man. And let me tell ya, Satan ain't an easy boss to please."

Arnold nodded his head. "Yeah, if he were real, I'd have to guess you're right."

"Us demons, the *worker* demons that is, we don't have the same privileges as the better-known guys. Our names aren't household, you see? We're not Succubi or Incubi or anything special like that." He snorted, a small flame shooting from his nostril that filled the air with the smell of freshly burned matches. "We're just the ones who keep Hell from falling apart. That's all. No big deal."

"O…kay?"

"The big guys, they can come and go as they please. Roam around on this strange and fucked up planet, any dimension they want, too, and at any time. Plus, they get summoned by you dumbass humans all the time just to have hot orgies and shit. Us little guys, we never get to have any fun. We just get sent out to the shit jobs. You know, trying to tempt little kids to kill their pets and take God's name in vain. Once in a great while, *if* we're lucky, we may get tasked with the job of bringing in a soul, but it's never a good soul. Never one of the mass murderers or cult leaders or anything. And do you know the odds of a little demon like me getting a promotion?"

Arnold shrugged. "Yeah, I have no idea, man. I didn't even realize that demons got promotions. Hell, I didn't realize they even had to hold down jobs."

"Oh yeah, we do. Most humans don't realize it. That's because you guys are more worried about yourselves than what's going on around you. Even God hates humans, man. You know that, right?"

"God? No way. God created us in *His* image. Says so in the Bible. God loves us. I mean, if it were all real, he would love us. He'd have to. That's one of the whole biblical fallacies. Kinda funny, really"

"*Bible*? Ha!" Arraleg let out a boisterous laugh; one that, if coming from someone of a more normal human size, would have deafened Arnold. "The Bible was written by humans! Trust me, buddy, you guys may think you follow Jesus and God and all that bullshit, but I've actually *talked* with him. He's real, and so am I, and so is Satan."

Arnold didn't know how to respond. He was still stuck on the fact that he was standing naked in his bathroom talking to a miniature action-figure sized red demon. Maybe he had been wrong all this time. Maybe God and Satan and Heaven and Hell *were* real.

"But anyway, back to my story. The odds are horrible."

"Huh," Arnold said. "Odds? Odds of what?"

"Were you even listening to me? For fuck's sake, man."

Arnold nodded gently, slightly embarrassed. "Oh, yeah. Sorry. I was just thinkin'."

Arraleg stretched his neck and shrugged. "It's okay. You're only human, right?" He grinned. "But the odds, as I was saying, of a demon like me getting a promotion…they aren't good at all. So, I decided I wanted to take a little vacation, and I just bolted. Ran for the hills, as you humans say. You know?"

Arnold listened to the little demon with deep interest. Not so much because he believed him, though he was starting to have doubts about his own ideology, but he was a good story teller. And, no matter what he believed anyway, whoever or *whatever* the little guy actually was, he had climbed out of his ear for cryin' out loud. That was definitely strange and different, to say the least.

"Yeah. Sounds like you had it rough down there in…" he cleared his throat, nearly unable to bring himself to say the word. It was ridiculous, wasn't it? Hell? Real? "Well, uhm, *Hell*, I guess."

"Don't worry. I know what you're thinking. If I ain't proof enough for you, what's gonna happen soon will do more than make you see the truth."

"What do you mean?"

"He's gonna come after me. Would've already got me if I didn't take cover in the first hiding place I found. Now that I'm out, he'll be able to find me pretty easily when I start doin' what I have to do."

"What? Who's gonna come after you?"

"Satan."

"Yeah? Well what's that got to do with m —" Arnold's mind locked like an ungreased and rusted gear. *Had to take cover…but, he was in my…*

Arraleg reared back and pointed to Arnold's head. "Yep. Now you're startin' to put it together."

Holy shit.

"That's right, *Jack*. I jumped inside your head to mask myself. Worked pretty good, too."

"But, you're out now. You're free to go. Right?"

"Well, I'm out, yeah. But he don't care about that. He'll get me. He always does. Others have tried to escape in the past, I just made it farther than most. When he does get me, he's gonna want the soul of anyone who aided and abetted. Free to go, though…not just yet."

For the first time in forever, Arnold felt a genuine wave of fear cascade over his body. His stomach dropped and his fingers turned to ice. The ultimate question, the one that every person asks at some point in their life, sprang to his mind.

What if?

What if everything Arraleg was saying was actually true? He swallowed hard, his nerves finally getting to him. "Aided and abetted? You mean helped you? What do you mean? I didn't help you! I certainly don't intend to aid and abet anyone or anything!"

The little demon bared his teeth, his eyes squinted to tiny black slits in a sea of red, almost flaming skin. "Well, you *kinda* did."

"I didn't *help* you. What kind of a person do you take me for? I'd never help a demon. I mean…if they were real, I wouldn't."

"Well you did, brother. Gave me a place to crash and hide out for a few days."

"Well leave! Jesus, man. Let's just stop for a minute and think about this. If Satan were to be real, I certainly wouldn't want him coming to take my soul all because some little shit demon started hangin' around! No offense, but you've caused me enough trouble with my ear for the last week or so."

"What's the matter?" Arraleg's head bent to the side, a *devilish* grin stretched across his thin, red lips. "Thought you didn't *believe* in me?"

"Oh, shut up. Just go! Get the hell outta here and go back to wherever it is you came from."

"Well, like I was trying to tell you a minute ago, I'm afraid I can't. Not just yet, anyway. You see, I'm bound by the code of demons, now. I've gotta honor that before I'm free."

"Code of demons? You've gotta be kidding me. Demons follow a *code*?"

Arraleg jumped up and started pacing back and forth on the sink. "Yep. Believe it or not, demons go by a code, too. Only a couple of rules, but we gotta stick to them no matter what. The first one goes like this. When some of the big guys are trying to possess your kind, if the human can trick the demon into causing actual physical harm to them or their family, then that demon belongs to the human for the rest of the human's life."

A sudden rush of cold air whished across Arnold's testicles reminding him that he was still naked. "Hmm. So, does that mean that you guys aren't allowed to hurt us?"

Arraleg nodded. "That's right. Most people think we can do some real damage, but the almighty won't allow it. Apparently, humans are pussies. They always act and talk all big and bad and shit, but if you cause them the slightest bit of pain or discomfort, they usually give in and do whatever you ask. God doesn't like that we can just manipulate them so easily with pain. He says that if we want a human soul, we gotta fool them in a smart way. Fucking ridiculous if you ask me." He shook his head. "Nobody wants to be a slave to a…" He trailed off, looked up at Arnold with a sort of mocking grin. "Well, you get the idea. That's not relevant in this case. Here, with me and you, it's the second rule that applies."

"Oh? And what is that?"

The little demon looked at Arnold as seriously as he possibly could. "If a human grants refuge to, or helps in any way, a demon, whether the human is aware of it or not, the demon then owes said human three wishes."

A surprised look overtook Arnold. "Oh. Wishes, huh?" He walked over to the toilet and sat down. A thousand things were running through his mind at this point. Up until a few brief moments ago, he would have simply shrugged everything Arraleg had said off as just another story. Not anymore. Now, he had a vested interest, *and*, he was actually worried. The shower was still running and the room was now enveloped in a thick layer of steam. "You mean that, because I helped you, even though I didn't want to or know about it…Satan will come to get me? And you can't leave because I did unknowingly help you, and also for that same reason, you now owe me three wishes?"

"That's right. I *have* to do it, whether I want to or not. It's in the demon's handbook. If I don't, I have to become your slave until you die, at which time,

I will die too. Otherwise, Satan will see to it that I am no more. And trust me, neither of those options sound particularly appealing."

"Three wishes? You're shittin' me, man. There's no way you can grant wishes. That stuff is just make-believe. You know, kid's stories. Aladdin and his lamp and all that."

"Ah, yes. Aladdin. He was a nice guy."

Arnold stared at the demon, bewildered.

"Jesus H. Christ!" Arraleg exclaimed, bursting with laughter. "You humans believe anything! Of course I didn't know Aladdin. That shit is fake as fuck. Goddamn, son."

Arnold wiped his face and took a deep breath. "So…you're just bullshittin' me then? The whole thing…you're just bullshittin'?"

Arraleg slapped his hand against his forehead and sighed. "Look dumbass, I'm gonna just lay it out for you all at once, and in the simplest way I can. You ready to actually listen this time?"

Arnold nodded the way a kindergartener would when being explained the rules to a simple game.

"Okay. I am a demon. I ran away from Hell. Satan is going to come after me. I hid inside of your head to mask my presence. That means you helped me. Demon code states that, because you provided me refuge, I have to grant you three wishes. Good so far?"

Arnold's eyes squinted, his mouth slightly open, and he nodded again.

"Great. Now, Satan will come after me. He's probably looking right now, and he *will* find me. When he does, he will punish me in a very bad way, and he will also punish you and take your soul for helping me."

"But—" Arnold started.

"I'm not done yet," Arraleg interjected. "Why are humans so rude?" He gave Arnold the side-eye and continued. "But, there's a catch."

"A catch?" Arnold said, a slight glint of hope returning to his voice.

"There's *always* a catch. Satan will let you go, and he will grant me entry back into Hell, unharmed, *if* I bring him a sufficient sacrifice."

"A sacrifice? You mean, like…a goat or something?"

The little demon fell silent. He stared at Arnold with dumb amusement. "No. Just…no. Not a goat. That's just something that was made popular by human entertainment companies in movies and shit. Turns out, Satan doesn't really care about all the ritualistic sacrifices and all that. Plus, he absolutely hates being associated with goats. All he wants are souls. *Human* souls. And you know, he doesn't even want them for the reasons that most Christians think."

"Oh?"

"Yeah. He likes to collect souls along with the bodies they came in and have sex with them. Brutal, hardcore, wild and rough sex. I'm talking big daddy demon gangbangs and torture porn type of sex. The whole thing's also a big pissing contest between him and God. Who has the most souls and such. Pathetic, really. But, I digress." He arched his head to the side and cupped a hand over his ear. "Sounds like you're about to have a visitor."

Arnold's eyes widened. "Satan?"

"No, dummy. Fuck's sake. Mary is on her way."

"Mary? Oh *shit*. I've not even been in the shower yet! Hey man, give me a minute, will you? Let me jump in and get my hair wet. That way it'll at least *look* like I showered."

"Yeah, sure. Like she'll even care. Based on the way she was treating you earlier, I don't think she'd care if you just up and left."

Arnold stopped and looked to the floor. "That's just how she is. She loves me, man. Trust me. I know she does."

"Yeah, yeah. Whatever you gotta keep tellin' yourself to get through, pal. Take it from me though, she checked out of the relationship a long time ago. Probably fucking somebody else too, if I had to guess. I've had a lot of experience in that department for work, you know." He looked Arnold up and down, pointing at his groin with a laugh. "Based on the size of *that* thing, I wouldn't blame her."

"What? What *thing*?" Arnold said, confused.

Arraleg stared at his crotch, his eyebrows raised.

"Wait…you mean…you think that she acts this way because of my —"

"All I'm sayin' is, it ain't helpin' you any to have a micro pee pee."

Arnold thought back to when Mary had first started acting the way she does now. When they first met, they were having sex daily, at *least*. Nowadays, she hardly looked at or spoke to him, let alone touched him. What Arraleg was saying actually made sense for once. Maybe Mary was fucking someone else. She did talk a lot about her guy friends…*Brian* specifically came to mind. But having a small penis wasn't the reason, was it? She didn't seem to mind when they'd first met. Sure his dick was on the low side of average...but it wasn't *micro* by any stretch of the imagination. Besides...it ain't the size that matters...is it?

"That's crazy. Even if she *was* fucking someone else, and I'm not saying she is, just *if* she was, size doesn't matter. And anyway, it's not like I can change it. Sort of stuck with what you got, you know?"

"Mmm...that's not necessarily true. You do have three wishes now, remember?"

Arnold looked down in shame at his shriveled member, then eyed his demon friend. "You mean..."

"Your wish is my command, big daddy."

"I don't know if I should. I mean—"

"She's coming. She can't find out about me, either. The less humans that know about me, the better. I'll be back when you can catch a free minute to chat. Anytime she's not around, you just say my name and I'll pop out."

"Okay. I guess I better get in the shower then."

"Yep. Better hurry. She'll be here in, three, two, one..."

The bathroom door opened and a rush of cold air blasted into the room.

PART III

THE TRUTH SHALL
SET YOU FREE

8

MARY THREW THE DOOR OPEN AND STEPPED INTO THE DENSE FOG. "Damn, Arnie! Are you alive in there somewhere? You've been here a while."

Arnold scrambled to wet his body. He held his hands directly under the water and ran them over his balding head, soaking what little hair he had left before pulling the shower curtain back enough to see. "Just showering. Took a little longer than I expected."

Mary raised her eyebrows and eyed his body up and down through the steam. Her gaze stopped at his groin, a slight smirk evident on her face. "Well, you don't have much hair left, and it's not like you have a lot to clean, you know. Can't imagine it taking you *that* long."

"What's that supposed to mean?" Arnold looked at his penis again, self-conscious of her seemingly well-chosen words.

"Oh, nothing. It just means what it means."

"Yeah? Well why did you look that way at my *dick* when you said it? Huh? You think my cock is too small? That why you never pay any attention to me anymore?" He drew back, embarrassed at himself, at how he'd let his usually restrained emotions get the better of him.

Mary scrunched her face. "What in the *hell* are you talking about?" She walked over to the shower and pulled the curtain to the side, exposing his flaccid penis.

He stood, frozen in place as it dangled before him like a tiny little limp noodle, water dripping from the tip. "I, uhm, I don't…"

Unable to control herself, Mary started to laugh. "Why would I not pay attention to you because of the size of *that*?"

"Well, I, uh —"

"What you *really* wanna know is why haven't we fucked in a while, right? You wanna know if I've moved on to *bigger* and, uhm, *better* things. Is that what this little outburst is about?"

"Uh, w…well…I mean, it has been a while since we've —"

Mary snorted. "Your dick *is* pretty small, though. But, I mean, not like you can help it. *If* that was the reason, that is." She turned around and started for the door.

"What? The reason for what? Does that mean that —"

"I just came to tell you I'm going out for a while, Arnold. Goin' out to meet Brian for a *work* thing." She turned around just before closing the door.

"Really, Arnold. It's not your fault. The penis thing, you know. Some are blessed with larger parts than others. Take your time in there, I'll bet your hand won't be able to tell the difference."

"Mary! Mary, wait!" Arnold rushed to turn the water off and get out of the shower in time to catch her, but it was too late. She'd already started pulling out of the driveway by the time he'd gotten out of the shower, thrown on a towel, and made it to the front door. He tried calling her, but every time he hit her name it went straight to voicemail. "Fuck!" He sat on the bed and began to cry. Things used to be so good between them, and for the life of him, he couldn't figure out where everything had gone wrong. "Meeting *Brian* for a work thing, huh? I'll bet. *Work*, my ass. Jesus, Mary. I *love* you!"

"What you cryin' about, big guy?"

The voice startled Arnold. He jumped to his feet, yelping like a hurt pup. "Oh, it's just you."

"Hey, now. Just because I was right about your less than faithful slut bag of a wife is no reason to be mean to *me*. Demons have feelings too, you know."

"What did I do wrong?" Arnold pleaded. "I don't understand it. I did everything for her. *Everything*. And now she's off somewhere fucking Brian? *Brian*, of all people. Goddamn fucking *Brian*! Fuck!"

"Yeah. It's always tough for you guys to hear things like that. I've been the cause of a lot of it. Playing games with human feelings and shit. It can be a bit of fun on occasion. In the demon world, everybody sort of just has sex with everybody else. Nobody really cares. Kinda eliminates all the problems associated with it. Humans are strange in that way. All that monogamy bullshit."

"She didn't even say why," Arnold sobbed. "I love her, man. What am I supposed to do? She's my everything!" He bent over and started to ugly cry, his face contorting into an image reminiscent of a glob of melting silly putty.

Arraleg hopped up on the bed next to him and gave him a friendly pat on the leg. "Women. Hard to please 'em, especially the human variety. Unless you have a massive cock, that is." He chuckled. He just couldn't help himself. "I'm sorry, buddy. Really. Listen…you might not have one now, but I can rectify that problem for you in a matter of seconds. All you have to do is wish it to be."

"Don't you even care? She broke my heart!" Snot and tears leaked down onto Arnold's lips, a disgusting mess making even the little demon wince.

He shook his head. "Right. And I just told you how to fix it. I really don't think I'll ever get used to how fucking stupid your species is. What did I say? Oh, that's right! Wish for a bigger dick and I'll make it happen! Then, she'll never wanna fuck another guy again. Trust me. It's all about the D. This won't be the first time I'll have granted that wish, and I guarantee it won't be the last…unless Satan kills me, that is. Then it will. But it works."

Arnold raised his head, a brief lapse in the snot-filled, gagging cries. "You think that'll really work?"

Arraleg nodded. "Yep. If all you want is for her to fuck you, it will. Works every time."

"Really?"

"Yep. Women love the D, man. Especially when they're big. But—"

"I wish for a bigger dick, then!" Arnold shouted. "Make my dick, eight inches long. And make it *thick*, too! That'll give her somethin' to stay with me for!"

"Fuck, man. You didn't let me finish what I was about to say. If all you want is for her to fuck you, then that's definitely the answer. But if you want her to *love* you, that's different. We aren't allowed to grant wishes of love." He looked at Arnold and snapped his fingers. "But you already wished it, so it has to be now. No goin' back."

"You mean that she won't—"

Arnold shifted in the bed. He scooted to the right, then to the left, squirming the way a dog does when it has to take a shit but struggling to wait until it can go outside. "Holy shit. Something's happening."

"Well, yeah. I told you. Your wish is my command."

Wide eyed, Arnold looked down at the towel wrapped around his waist. Slowly, something beneath it began to push the fabric up. He felt a strange sensation between his legs, one he'd never felt before. It was similar to an orgasm, but very different at the same time. This was a feeling of great pleasure, yet not as explosive and all-encompassing as that sudden release of built-up emotion and dominating power from climaxing.

"I-is it—"

"Take a look for yourself."

Arnold took the towel in his hands and pulled it up with extreme delicacy. He stood up, a huge smile on his face, and dropped the towel to the floor. "Holy fucking *shit*! How did you do that?" He turned to Arraleg. "What the fuck, man? This is amazing!"

"Yeah, yeah. I know. I'm a miracle worker," the little demon bragged with a smirk.

Arnold was in absolute awe of what hung between his thighs. His cock, which had been an average but meager four and a half to five inches erect on a good day only seconds ago, was now a whopping eight inches. And that was *soft*! And to top it all off, it was now as thick as a television remote. "How did you...shit man!" He took his member in hand, flipping it back and forth as excitedly as a child on Christmas morning.

"Just wait 'till that wife of yours gets a look at that big boy. You guys'll be fuckin' all night long."

"I just, I just can't believe this is real." Arnold stared at his newly enlarged penis, twirling it around like a helicopter propeller. "A...and, it'll work? I mean, everything else is the same?"

"Yep. Just like it always was. You just have a respectably sized dick now."

Arnold began to cry, only this time, he cried tears of pure joy.

9

WHEN MARY CAME THROUGH THE FRONT DOOR A FEW HOURS LATER, the sight of her naked husband laying on the couch caught her by surprise. "Arnold? What in the hell are you do-holy *shit*!" She stopped, dead in her tracks, and stared at him. Her eyes stretched wide, her mouth fell open, an audible gasp escaped from the pit of her stomach.

Arnold lay on his side, his head propped on one hand, the other hand twirling his newly enlarged cock in circles as if it were a lasso. "Like it?"

"What the hell? Is...is that thing *real*?"

He smiled at her and slid his hand up and down the shaft. "Yep. And it's all yours, baby."

Mary walked over to him, crouched next to his groin, and examined his cock. "What happened to it? I mean, earlier today it wasn't like this." She looked into his eyes, awe and confusion clutching her tight in its grasp. "Can I...*touch* it?"

"Ha! Of course, you can touch it, Mary! You're

my wife!"

Her eyes gleamed with a long-forgotten brightness. She went to her knees and leaned in close, her hand hovering only millimeters from his skin. She was so close she could feel the warmth radiating from him as fresh blood filled the massive muscle, priming it for its one true and intended purpose. Her smile grew even larger, stretching nearly from ear to ear. "My *God*," she whispered. "How did you do this? How did you get it to be so big?"

"I just sort of, wished it into being, I guess. Go on. Touch it. It's waiting."

She took his now fully erect cock in her hand and lightly stroked the shaft, a giggle escaping her mouth as she licked her lips hungrily. She looked up into Arnold's eyes and winked. "Get ready, *big* boy." She turned her face back toward his genitals and lowered her lips close to the head of his penis, gently exhaling warm breath onto it.

Arnold groaned and arched his back.

"Dear, Lord," she whispered. "It's even bigger than Bri…" She jerked back, her hand flew to her mouth, covering it. She looked up at Arnold, who was now staring back at her, his mouth hanging open, eyes large and surprised.

He raised up, supporting his weight on his elbows. "What did you just say?"

Mary shook her head. "Nothing. I just said your so *big*." She smiled stupidly.

"Yeah. I heard that. Bigger than *who*, though?" His face was red, his cock turning limp as blood rushed away from it and to other parts of his body. "Were you going to say Brian?" He scooted back to a seated position on the end of the couch.

Flustered, Mary struggled to regain composure. "Arnold, no! Are you crazy?" She took a seat on the opposite end of the couch, her eyes darting back and forth from Arnold to the door and to the floor. "Brian and I, it's all just business. Work, you know?"

He watched her closely as she attempted to explain, noticing that her hands were shaking now. Her breaths short and rapid. "Really? So, you weren't going to say his name, then? You've never slept with him or seen his cock?"

Mary's face fell flat for a brief moment before returning to a forced smile. "Arnold, you're losing your mind. You know I'd never do that to you." She lowered her head slightly, looking up at Arnold, her lower lip pouting out.

Arnold glanced across the room to Mary's purse. She'd dropped it next to the door when her attention had been taken by his porn-star like appendage. "Okay. Then you won't mind if I check your phone, will you?" He jumped up and darted across the room, snatching her purse.

"Arnold, wait! Put that down right now!" She tried to sprint to him and knock the bag from his hands, but banged her shin on the table. "Arnold, stop it! You can't even unlock it!"

He took her phone from the bag and pressed the home key. The screen lit up. There were several unread texts listed, the majority of them from Brian. "I know your password, Mary." He punched it in and opened the texts. "Okay, let's see what *Brian* has to say. 'Had a nice time tonight. Don't forget to shower before getting in bed with that *loser* husband of yours, *wink wink*...'. What the fuck, Mary?

How long has this been going on?"

"Arnold," she said, limping over to him as her shin throbbed. "It's not what you think. It was hot in the office. We, I mean, I got sweaty."

"Yeah, I bet you did," he said, scrolling through the text thread. "This is probably why. He held the phone up and read the message aloud, 'Happy my cock makes you smile…'." Looking down at his wife, his lips began to quiver, his eyes welled with tears. "I've done everything for you, Mary. *Everything*! And this is how you repay me?" He threw the phone across the room and stormed off toward the bedroom.

"Arnold, wait. Just wait a minute. I'm sure we can figure something out! I love you, too, baby! Come back and let's make up, please? We can figure this out!"

His hand on the bedroom door, Arnold turned to her and snorted. "Goddamn, Mary. You don't *love* me. You love big dicks! That's all! It's obvious now. You're nothing but a cock-thirsty whore who jumps on the biggest swingin' dick in town!"

"Oh, *fuck* you, Arnold! I'm sick of your fucking little whiny ass 'I'm never good enough for anything beg me just to *fuck* you' attitude. Yeah, I *was* fucking Brian! There, you happy? I fucked him just a little while ago, in fact, and it was *amazing*! Ten-times better…no, a thousand times better than any sex I've ever had with you!"

Arnold slumped against the door frame his heart shattering from the verbal onslaught.

Mary took a deep breath and laughed, holding her hand in front of her as she gestured to him. "You see? This, for Christ's sake. This is a big reason why

I did it! Look at you. You're not a man. You're a goddamn little whiny bitch! No woman want's that in a partner. Fuck!"

"Stop Mary. Just stop!" he cried, crouching down in the doorway of the bedroom.

"Fuck this." She walked over and grabbed her phone. "You know, it's too bad you can't grow some balls with that nice new big dick of yours so you can use it right. I'm going to Brian's. *Maybe* I'll be back in the morning after another good *fuck* calms me down!"

"Mary!" Arnold cried as she slammed the door. "Mary!"

"Well, it *was* working, until all that shit happened."

Arnold looked over and saw Arraleg sitting on the floor in front of him. "Did you hear her? She cheated on me…with *him*."

"Yep, I heard. Don't try and act like you didn't already know it was happening, man. Like I said before…women. Ha!"

"I just don't know what I'm gonna do without her. We've been together for so long."

The little demon walked over and placed his hand on Arnold's naked leg. "Well, if I may, I'd suggest putting on some pants, at least. I don't wanna see you walking around all naked and shit."

Arnold cracked a faint smile.

"That's better, buddy." He patted Arnold's leg. "I've got something that I *know* will make you feel better. I'll tell you first thing in the morning. Tonight, you rest. Trust me, you're gonna need it." The little demon winked at him, a smile on his face. "Now, how 'bout those pants, huh?"

10

ARNOLD WOKE TO THE SMELL OF BACON AND EGGS. It'd been a long time since he'd woken to that smell. In fact, he couldn't even begin to remember the last time it'd happened. The sun was shining in through the bedroom window and he threw his hand over, feeling for Mary.

She wasn't there.

He frowned. *Fuck. I guess it wasn't just a nightmare.*

"Good morning!" Arraleg came into the room, a tray filled with toast, fried eggs, bacon, and orange juice magically hovering in the air behind him. "You ready to start the day fresh, big guy?" He waved his hand, floating the tray of food over to the bed and gently sitting it down.

"You didn't have to do this, man. Really."

"Oh, now. I wanted to. After all, you had a pretty rough night."

Arnold scratched his head and took a piece of toast and bacon from the tray. "Yeah. I remember." He glanced to his new friend as sadness filled his eyes. "She didn't come back?"

"Afraid not. But she will. Probably, anyway."

"How do you know that?"

Arraleg jumped up on the bed. "Because, they always do. She got a glimpse of that massive cock you're packin', and I've seen enough of her type to know that she is *exactly* what you called her last night."

"Huh? What did I call her?"

The demon laughed. "You mean you don't re-member?" He stared at Arnold for a moment. It was obvious the human didn't have a clue. "Well, brace yourself. You called her a cock-thirsty whore who jumps on the biggest swingin' dick around. Somethin' like that."

"Christ. No wonder she didn't come back."

"Relax, man. That had nothing to do with her leaving. It was inevitable. Bound to happen sooner or later. Good thing is, there are plenty of fish in the sea, as you guys say."

Arnold swallowed the last of his breakfast and drank his juice down. "I don't know. Not really sure I wanna replace her. You know?"

Arraleg's eyes widened. "What's wrong with you? You really are pussy-whipped. Goddamn!"

"No, I just…I love her."

"Well, she doesn't love you. And just think, what good is a nice new package when you can't even use it?"

Arnold glanced down to his lap. It had been a long time for him. He'd jerked off, sure, but he longed for that sweet release of another human. He needed it. But it'd been even *longer* since he'd put any effort into meeting someone, and that thought made him nervous. "I mean, I guess. But I don't know that I'd even be able to meet anybody. I mean, where do people even go nowadays to do that kinda shit? Online?"

His demon friend grinned. "You just leave that part to me. If you really and truly want women, all you have to do is wish it, remember?"

"I want Mary to love me again."

Arraleg shook his head. "I'm afraid that one's not gonna happen. And even if I *wanted* to grant that wish, it's not within my power, remember? Did we not talk about this? One of the few rules to this whole wish thing."

Arnold's face suddenly lit up as a thought came to him. "But, maybe if there's a woman here when she comes back, maybe she'll get jealous. Yeah... *yeah*! That could work, right?"

"You're really bad off, you know that?"

"Right?"

"Look, man. I've seen stranger things happen, I guess. But I'm telling you now, she doesn't love you and she never will. Women, I can give you. Love, I can't."

"Yeah. That's it then. I want women. I want them to really *want* me. To *lust* for me. That'll show her." He stood up and grabbed a fresh pair of pants. "I'm gonna go take a shower."

"So that's your wish then? For women?"

"Yeah. Women. That'll make her jealous enough. Be out in a minute."

"Hey, just one question first. What's your type?

89

You know, what type of women do you prefer?"

"I don't know. Hot ones! Just surprise me." He went into the bathroom and turned on the shower. He pulled his pants down, tossing them to the side, and pulled the shower curtain back to get in. As he raised his leg, he felt a soft touch lay against his hip. Suddenly, the sweet scent of vanilla filled the air and a soft, sultry voice floated into his ear.

"Mind if I join you, sexy?"

Startled, he jumped away from the sensation, quickly turning to see what was going on. "Holy hell! Where did you come from?"

Standing in front of him was a thing of pure beauty. The young woman was no taller than five and a half feet, her hips and chest thick and busty. Long, curly, dirty blond hair draped from her head, her lips full and pink, contrasting perfectly against her pale, silky smooth skin.

"That doesn't really matter, does it?" she said, rubbing a nipple with one hand, the other massaging her naked and hairless vagina. "All that matters is that I'm here now." She glanced down at Arnold's penis, now erect and bouncing up and down in perfectly timed pulses. She bit her lower lip. "So, how about it?"

A large smile stretched across his face. "I mean, I don't have a problem with it. If you're sure you want to, that is. I don't wanna force you to do anything."

The woman closed her legs together and bent her knees, dipping down and then up again. "Not only do I *want* to…I *need* to." She pressed her body against his, sliding her tongue between his lips as she kissed him.

He closed his eyes and drifted off into sheer ecstasy. Her touch was maddening, a thing of absolute and unadulterated pleasure. He heard something in the room behind her and when he cracked his eyes, he saw three more naked beauties. He pulled away from the woman he was kissing. "What is this?"

Before him stood the most luscious and sexy women he'd ever seen. The dirty blond he'd already met was now accompanied by a sultry redhead, a brunette with the naughtiest look on her face, and a platinum blond that was to die for.

"We heard you like all types of women," the redhead said. "It's always best to cover the bases."

"That's right," the naughty brunette said. "And we wanna cover *all* of the bases."

"We just want to play," the platinum blond murmured. "That's all. One-hundred percent all play, all the time."

The smile on his face was larger and more genuine than it had been in years. "Arraleg," he whispered. "You dirty little devil."

PART IV

A DIFFERENT KIND OF DEVIL

II

WHEN THE GROUND FIRST STARTED TO SHAKE, Arnold didn't know what was happening. He was in the middle of his bed, scores of beautiful, naked women laying around and on top of him, and he'd just drifted off to sleep after hours of the nastiest most exhilarating sex of his life.

"What was that?" he mumbled, raising his head. "A...Arraleg? That you? You doin' that?" There was no response. One of the women next to him shifted position, her hand sliding down and hugging his cock, forcing him to grin. "Arraleg?"

The ground quaked again, this time with enough presence to knock pictures from the walls. He raised up and climbed over the passed-out women. "What the fuck? Arraleg? Is that you?"

Once again, the ground shook, this time with even more intensity. He ran over to the window and peered outside. "Holy *shit*!" he screamed. In his back yard, a narrow gap had formed in the earth, swallowing an oak tree that had been there since before he'd bought the place.

Arraleg came rushing into the room, panting like a fat kid running stair repeats. "He's found us! We gotta do something, quick!"

Arnold spun around. "What? Who found us? What's happening?"

"It had to have been the magic, the wishes. He was able to narrow in on my location because of it. He knows. It's Satan…he's coming, and he's gonna take both of us if we don't get him that sacrifice, fast!"

"You're kiddin'?" He turned back to the window.

The gap had widened, now every bit of ten feet across. From inside, flames roared, scorching the tips of the grass around the opening.

"This is crazy!" Arnold shouted. "It can't be happening!"

A hand emerged from the fire, pulling behind it a tall, thin bodied man. He was dressed very differently than Arnold had ever imagined Satan would dress. What he'd always pictured was the stereotypical devil in human form portrayed in movies. Black suit, shined shoes, slick hair, and most of all, attractive. The man coming from inside the ground didn't have any of those characteristics.

He wore a striped suit that was colored like a rainbow, and his feet were adorned with a pair of pink flip-flops. His head was bald, except for a horribly placed combover that stretched from just above his right ear. His ears were so large that they reminded Arnold of the old-style satellite dishes.

The only thing that looked even vaguely *devil like* was the color of his skin, and even that was more like the old cartoon devils; a dull shade of red. Sort of like Arraleg's skin.

"Are you fucking kidding me?" Arnold said as he burst out laughing. "*That* is the person you're afraid of? Look at him! He looks like a goddamn weirdo!"

Arraleg ran into the bathroom and hid under the sink. "You better hide, man! He's rougher than he looks, I'm tellin' you!"

The sound of the doorbell chimed through every room and Arnold burst out laughing. "Seriously? He rings the fucking doorbell? Ha!"

"No! Don't! He'll kill us all!"

"From the looks of it, this guy couldn't even kill himself." Arnold opened the door to greet the strange man with a big smile on his face. "Can I help you?"

The man returned the smile, his lips rather thin and horribly chapped. "Well, hello there." He held out his hand in a polite gesture. "I do believe you have something that belongs to me." His voice was high pitched, very similar in tone to Arraleg's, but with a more feminine touch. Maybe it was a demon thing?

Arnold looked at the extended hand. Like the rest of his body, the skin was red. Each of his fingers were tipped in a long, sharply pointed claw. "Holy fuck. Look at those things."

The man's eyes shifted from Arnold to his fingernails, then back again. "It's impolite to refuse the hand of someone when offered. Regardless of the state of their *nails*."

"Oh yeah." Arnold took his hand and shook it. It was very dry and rough to the touch. "I'm sorry, I don't think we've met. My name is—"

"Arnold," the man interrupted. "Arnold Masterson."

"Uhm...okay. How did you know that?"

"I know all about you, Mr. Masterson. I know *all* things."

Arnold pulled his hand back and started to wipe it on his pants, but realized that he was still naked. "Oh, shit. Sorry...I just, uh, well."

The man continued to smile, looking down at Arnolds limp prick. "Yes. You have him, the one who belongs to me. That is obvious."

"Excuse me?" Arnold said, covering his dick. "What is that supposed to mean?"

"Well," the man said. "That thing between your legs is quite a bit larger than what it *should* be. It's obviously the work of a special little demon with the power to grant wishes. Tell me, Mr. Masterson, does the name *Arraleg* ring any bells?"

Arnold swallowed hard. He was nervous now. The man hadn't looked that scary from the window, but now that he was there, standing in front of him, there was just something about his presence that seemed overly disturbing. "No. What kind of a name is that, anyway?"

The man nodded calmly. "Allow me to explain a bit further, Arnold. I may call you that, I assume?"

Arnold stared at him, unsure of what to say.

"Yes, I'll call you that. Anyway, I am the one you humans blame for all of your troubles. I go by many names, though most were given to me by those who are not my father. The one you very likely know me by is Satan."

His hands started to tremble; small tremors, nearly unnoticeable to the human eye.

"I understand," Satan said. "That happens a lot more than you'd imagine. It seems I'm a bit intimidating. I've no idea why."

"I don't know what you're talking about. I've never heard that name before. And as far as this thing goes," he grasped his dick in hand, "well Mr. Satan, I guess it's just how God made me. His image and all. I'm sure you can understand that."

Satan let out a boisterous laugh. "God doesn't do *that* kind of work, my friend. No, that is the work of little Arraleg. I'm rather certain of it." He raised his clawed hand and placed it on Arnolds chest, pushing him backward into the house. "Let me be clear. I *know* he is here. I know you helped him escape. Don't waste your time and breath even trying to lie to me."

"Look, man," Arnold protested. "I don't care who you are. You're not just gonna push your way into my house like some kind of thug!" He grabbed Satan's wrist and tried to push back, but the resistance was like trying to move a signpost out of a concrete base. He placed both hands around the wrist and tried harder, but a sudden sizzling sensation, one akin to placing a hand on a red-hot burner, flashed through his palms. "Jesus!" he screamed, pulling his hands away.

"Do not test me, *boy*," Satan protested. "I'm sure he explained the rules to you quite well. Either you provide me with an adequate soul for his sin, or I will punish him, and *you*, greatly." He pressed Arnold up against the wall, continuing to add pressure to his chest, restricting his breathing. "And I will use you as my own personal *sex* slave. Is that clear?" He pulled his hand back and Arnold fell to the ground.

"I really have no idea what you're talking about. I've never seen anything like that at a—"

Satan raised his hand and clenched it into a fist. As he did, Arnold's windpipe closed immediately. "Sure you don't, Arnold. Do you have a soul for my taking?"

Arnold grabbed his throat, the invisible force nearly too much.

"Oh, yes. Silly me," Satan said with a chuckle. He opened his hand and Arnold gasped for air.

"I'm seriou—"

Satan clenched his fist again, this time raising his hand in the air.

Arnold lifted with it, suspended in mid-air like a weightless ghost. His legs kicking for freedom as he struggled to breathe.

"Enough!" another voice yelled. "Let him go, please? It's not his fault."

Satan's focus went from Arnold, who was still hovering in the air, to the miniscule demon voice below him. "There you are," he said.

"Please, Satan, let the poor human go. He really had nothing to do with it."

"You told him the law, didn't you? The *rules*?"

"Well…yeah, bu—"

"Then he has everything to do with it." He dropped his hand allowing Arnold to fall again, his breath unrestricted once more.

"Take," he said, coughing. "Take one of them!" He pointed to the bedroom.

"No, Arnold," Arraleg yelled. "Just shut up!"

"You mean one of those cock hungry *sluts* brought about by this demon's granting of your childish little wish?"

Arnold looked at Satan and pleaded, "Yes! They're all yours! Take them all! Just leave us alone!"

Satan laughed again, shaking his head. "They have no souls, Arnold. They are but bodies used for one purpose; one emotion. Fuck toys, for *fucking*. They are beautiful for that, but it is the suffering I seek, not only the flesh." He knelt down, face to face to Arnold, and opened his mouth. Row after row of tiny jagged teeth covered every visible inch of his mouth and throat. A long, whip-like tongue slithered from deep within, sliding down into Arnold's body.

He choked again as Satan's tongue twisted down into his chest. It felt like something was being pulled from inside of his very core. His heart seized as if the demonic appendage had wrapped it up like a python does a rat. His hands found his chest, the only thing he could do was feel the immense pain.

In an instant, Satan withdrew his tongue. "Open your mouth with such foolish gibberish again and I'll rip it from your chest and eat it while you're still alive to watch."

"Just stop!" Arraleg yelled. "It was me who left, just take me back. I'll be your little bitch for all etern—"

"Wait!" Arnold shouted. "No. Don't take him back. I can get you what you want. I can bring you one, I just need a few minutes to talk to Arraleg. I need his help."

Satan hissed at him, a foul and rotten stench filling the air. "You want to make a deal with me, now? You do realize the consequences of such an endeavor?"

"I can bring you two, actually. One from a cold-hearted bitch, who, by chance, is also a cock-thirsty whore, and one from a self-centered and egotistical asshole with a cock almost as big as mine." He took a quick shot at his dick. "Well…not this big, but big nonetheless!"

Satan cocked his eyebrow, interest in his eyes. "Natural, or wished into existence like *that*," he asked, glancing to Arnolds loins.

"I mean, I don't know why it matters…but it's natural."

Satan's eyes gleamed with joy.

"But in return, I go free, and so does he." He pointed to Arraleg.

The little demon looked to Arnold, tears in his eyes. "You mean…"

"You want one of *my* demons in return for two ordinary human souls?" Satan asked him.

"No. Not just two ordinary souls. The soul of a cock-thirsty whore who'll spend her everlasting eternity pleasing her fiery cocked master, and the soul of a real fuckin' prick that you can use that same big ol' flamin' schlong on. Use them however you want! Shit, use them for the rest of eternity for all I care Fuck the shit outta them! All night long! But Arraleg gets to leave Hell for good!"

Satan looked at the little demon, who was now in tears. "This is quite an interesting proposition you present, and I'm not sure you can deliver.

But...I'll entertain it. I will return in exactly one hour, and you better deliver your end of the bargain." He stood to his feet and brought his hands together in a thunderous clap that filled the air with a thick smoke. When it cleared, Satan was gone.

Arraleg ran over and wrapped his little arms around Arnolds ankle. "You did that to save me?"

"Of course," Arnold said, staggering to his knees and lifting his friend in his hand. "You've been a great friend to me these past few days. You're the only one who's really been honest. The least I could do is try to get you away from Hell for good." He stood up and walked into the bedroom. Naked women still asleep all around, he chuckled. "If this works, I get to keep them, right?"

"Yep. Them *and* that big dick of yours."

"Great. Oh, and I know what my third wish is. Get that fucking bitch Mary over here, and have her bring Brian. They're in for a big surprise."

Arraleg smiled. "I like where this is going."

12

O KAY," ARRALEG SAID, LOOKING AT THE CLOCK ON THE WALL. "We've only got fifteen minutes left before Satan comes back. It's probably best to get them here just a little early to make sure something crazy doesn't happen."

"Yeah, okay. I agree with that."

"Remember, they're gonna be a little confused. They probably won't know where they are for a minute either, as I have no idea what they'll be doing when I work my magic. All I know for certain is that they'll be doing the same exact thing when they appear here. Got it?"

"Got it. You just get 'em here. We'll deal with everything else as it comes."

"Now, keep in mind, we have to *keep* them here. If they leave before Satan comes back, we're *all* fucked. And I don't mean like the way you fucked those sluts last night either. Got it?"

"Right," Arnold replied. "Keep 'em here."

"Whenever you're ready, wish it into existence, and I'll make it happen."

Arnold nodded, then lowered his head. "Arraleg, can I ask you a question real fast?"

"Sure man, but make it quick. Times a wastin'."

"Do you think she *ever* loved me? Like, even in the beginning?"

Arraleg thought for a bit before responding. "That's one I can't answer, buddy. What I can say, is that she wasn't always a cock-thirsty whore."

"Oh? What makes you think that?"

"Well, if we're being honest, your cock was pretty damn small before I did my thing." He laughed. "Wouldn't she just have went for something bigger from the get go if that were the case?"

"Not really," Arnold replied. "We used to fuck a lot. Like, five or ten times a day. She's *always* been cock-thirsty. She just started liking the big ones, I guess."

They both chuckled.

"Well, Arraleg, let's get this shitshow on the road. I wish for Mary, the cock-thirsty whore, and her new boyfriend Brian, the egotistical giant dicked menace, to be here in my living room."

Arraleg grinned and snapped his fingers. "Your wish is my command."

Arnold closed his eyes and took in a deep breath. At first, the quiet was pleasant. But it didn't last long. As he exhaled, the beautiful silence was replaced by an onslaught of wet slapping noises and loud moans and groans. He opened his eyes and saw his wife laying on the floor on her back, naked. On top of her was Brian, driving into her with a primal force.

"Fuck," Brian moaned. "Oh, fuck, I'm almost ready! I'm gonna cum!"

"Come on," Mary screamed. "Give it to m—" she opened her eyes and was immediately met with the stare of her husband. She screamed and started scooting on the floor, trying to push Brian off of her. "What the fuck!"

Brian opened his eyes just as he was about to explode deep inside of her. "What's wr—" He froze, confused. He rolled over and met Arnold's eyes as well. "What the fuck?"

"Hello there, *Brian*. Enjoying my wife, I see."

He looked around the floor for his clothes, but they were nowhere to be found. They'd been left in his apartment on the floor of his own bedroom. "What's happening?"

Mary continued to scream. She got to her feet and started toward the bedroom, but just as her hand met the door, she felt a sharp pain in her foot that caused her to fall.

"Take that, *bitch*!" Arraleg yelled, leaving a fresh bite mark on her ankle.

She screamed in terror and started scratching at the floor, trying to crawl away from the little demon.

Brian stood up, his large cock losing stiffness. "How the fuck? Where are we? What the fuck just happened?"

"Jesus," Arnold said to him. "Now I see why she started fucking you. Your dick is absolutely gigantic. I mean...for a normal human, that is." He smirked.

"Oh, thanks," Brian said, blushing. "I got lucky, I guess. Good genetics."

"Yeah, you might not wanna say that." Arnold looked at his watch. Less than a minute remained.

"Hey, what the fuck is goin' on here?" Brian said, still confused. "Why am I not still boning Mary?" He looked back to her. She was still on the floor screaming at Arraleg as he jumped up and down on her and made scary faces. "And what the fuck is that little thing?"

"Oh, that's my little demon friend, Arraleg."

Brian looked back at Arnold, a surprised smile on his face. "No way! That's cool as hell, dude."

"Yeah? Glad you think so." He looked at his watch. Ten seconds left. "Nine, eight, seven."

"Huh?"

"Four, three, two, one."

The front door burst open, slamming against the doorstop with authority. "Greetings, Mr. Masterson. Arraleg, my little minion demon. I expect you have what I—"

Mary continued to scream, the sounds drowning out Satan's voice.

"My *God*! Is that her? Is that the cock-thirsty whore you promised me?" He glanced at Arnold, who was nodding. He put his hand to his mouth and made a zipping motion. Mary's screams were immediately silenced as a set of metal zipper teeth appeared on her lips, closing them shut. "Silence, *woman*."

Brian let out an enormous cackle, pointing to Satan. "Look at this clown. What happened man? Circus leave you behind? Train leave without ya?"

Satan stared at him, his eyes settling on his dick.

"And this is the egotistical one with the massive dong you spoke of, I presume?"

"The very one," Arnold said. "They're here. I honored my half of the deal."

"Wait a minute," Brian said. "What deal. Who are you anyway, man? Some kind of clown?" He laughed at himself again, his ripped stomach flexing.

Satan shook his head in disgust. "You do realize that you just made that same joke, don't you?"

Brian continued to laugh.

Satan looked back to Arnold. "That one's dumber than a corn stalk, isn't he? Good thing he's hung like a horse."

"Hey man," Brian said. "Nobody calls me stupid and gets away with it. Especially not a damn clown!" He took a step toward Satan and drew his fist back, ready to plant one on his face.

Satan opened his mouth and roared at the human, the sound drastically different than his talking voice. He reached out and grasped Brian's dick, pulling him closer until they were nose to nose.

"Jesus, man! I'm sorry. I didn't mean anything bad!"

"This one will do just fine." He took a small wooden box from his pocket and opened it with his free hand. "This, my friend, is going to be your new home. The only time I'll let you out is when I feel like being pleasured. Do you understand?"

Brian laughed. "Hey man, you some kind of queerosexual or somethin'? Let go of my dick."

"I said, do you understand?"

"No way I'll fit in there. You're losing your mind."

A devilish grin fell on Satan's lips and he winked at Brian. Letting go of his cock, he brought a hand up between their faces and closed his forefinger and thumb together until they were about half an inch apart.

"What are you, anyway, some kind of…of…"

Brian began to shrink, his voice losing volume and tone as he went.

"Hey! What the fuck? What is this?" he squeaked.

Satan knelt down and picked the miniaturized man up, placing him in the box. He turned to Mary. She'd went silent now, shock stealing her voice. "Much better," Satan said to her. "My, you *are* quite the little cock-thirsty whore, aren't you?"

She shook her head and crawled to her feet, using the wall for support.

"Yes, you are. I can *smell* it. You're just covered in the scent of other men's semen. It smells *delicious*." He faced Arnold. "She was fucking around on you within the first year." He looked back to Mary. "You like the big ones, too. Well, you're in luck. Have a look at what you get now, anytime I want, for the rest of eternity." He dropped his pants down to his ankles and Mary gasped, along with everyone else in the room. Between Satan's legs hung what at first looked to be a giant meat log the size of a baseball bat. It was red, like the rest of his skin, the head rimmed with recurved spines. He winked at Mary. "You know what the best part is? I ejaculate flames."

"Told you," Arraleg said to Arnold. "I told you he could do that."

"Okay, that's enough of that," Satan said, pulling his pants back up. "This place, Earth, it isn't for me. Get in, dear." Just as he'd done to Brian, Satan shrunk Mary and placed her in the box.

"So…we're good?" Arnold asked. "We're free?"

"You know," Satan said. "The world paints me as a cruel, evil monster. I may do some bad things, but don't we all from time to time? There is one thing I am *not*, however, and that is someone who goes back on a deal. I've always, *always*, honored my deals. You have filled your end of the bargain, Mr. Arnold Masterson. So it shall be that I fulfill my end. You and the demon, Arraleg, are free to go."

Arraleg began to jump up and down with joy as he ran to his friend and hugged him.

"However, Mr. Masterson, you should know that, to deal with the devil is, in itself, a sin. You've really painted yourself into a corner for future endeavors, haven't you?"

Arnold took Arraleg in his palm and placed him on his shoulder. "We beat you once," he said to Satan, "and we'll be ready when you come back around."

He smiled at them, a look of mutual respect. "We'll see about that. Until then, enjoy your life. Hell can be a mighty lonely and hot place, you know." He stuck the box back in his pocket and clapped, again releasing a thunderous roar that filled the room with smoke before disappearing.

"He's right you know," Arraleg said. "You may end up in Hell after all in the end."

"No, *we* won't," he replied. "We'll figure it out. Besides, at least I got a big dick, some hot, sex addicted, soulless women who worship me, and a real friend out of the deal. I probably would've ended up in Hell anyway, except I'd have been miserable until then."

Arraleg laughed. "Glad you're seeing the positive side of things for a change."

"Yeah. I'll tell you, man, I'm sure happy you weren't a tumor or a bu…*fuck*!"

"What is it?" Arraleg asked.

"I just remembered the x-ray I had." He looked to Arraleg and laughed. "Doctor Roberts is gonna shit his pants when he sees you in there!"

Arraleg grinned. "Yep. Poor ol' bastard's gonna shit a goddamn brick."

Also By Tony Evans

Fourteen spine⬚tingling tales inspired by various urban legends and Appalachian folklore, all told in a classic Tales From the Crypt Style.

A collection of eight terrifying tales focusing on a darker side of Appalachia. A side where witches and ghosts linger in the shadows, waiting for that one unwary traveler. Come see for yourself⬚if you dare.

Appalachian witchery and black magic abound in this classic Appalachian witch tale. Fast paced and dark, these witches aren't for the faint of heart.

A satanic panic fueled gorefest about a teenage boy who encounters a secret satanic society, a demonic goat monster, and a hoard of savage, bloodthirsty insects in the mountains of eastern Kentucky.

Tony Evans is a crafter of horror and dark fiction, a spooky storyteller, and a lover of all things creepy. He is the author of over two-dozen short stories that have appeared in various print and online horror magazines and anthologies, two short story collections, two novellas, and one novel. Although Tony was born and raised in the Appalachian foothills of eastern Kentucky, he currently resides in New Albany, Indiana, where he spends his time coming up with bad storyideas, great dad jokes, and trying to entertain his wife and two young daughters – his favorite little monsters.

For a look into his daily life and to stay updated on all his fiction, current and new releases, and horror related projects, follow Tony on Twitter/Instagram:
@tonyevanshorror
or visit
TONYEVANSHORROR.COM

Made in the USA
Monee, IL
23 August 2022